# Crinkleroot's
## GUIDE TO KNOWING
# BUTTERFLIES & MOTHS
## BY JIM ARNOSKY

**Simon & Schuster Books for Young Readers**

**SIMON & SCHUSTER BOOKS FOR YOUNG READERS**
An imprint of Simon & Schuster Children's Publishing Division
1230 Avenue of the Americas, New York, New York 10020
Copyright © 1996 by Jim Arnosky
All rights reserved including the right of reproduction
in whole or in part in any form.
Simon & Schuster Books for Young Readers
is a trademark of Simon & Schuster.
The text for this book is set in ITC Bookman Medium.
The illustrations are rendered in watercolor.
Manufactured in the United States of America / First Edition
10 9 8 7 6 5 4 3 2 1

Library of Congress Cataloging-in-Publication Data
Arnosky, Jim.
Crinkleroot's guide to knowing butterflies and moths /
by Jim Arnosky.
1st ed.
p.   cm.
Summary : An illustrated introduction to the appearance
and habits of various butterflies and moths.
ISBN 0-689-80587-X
1. Butterflies—Juvenile literature.  2. Moths—Juvenile literature.
[1. Butterflies.  2. Moths.]  I. Title.
QL544.2.A76   1996   595.78—dc20                95-9408

FOR RODNEY, MICHELLE, AND DARREN

Hello. My name is Crinkleroot. I was born in a tree and raised by bees! I can speak caterpillar, moth, and butterfly, all at the same time. And I know every wild critter in the great outdoors!

Here on my hat is my friend snake. I call her Sassafrass. We're going to the wood's edge to look for butterflies. You can come too.

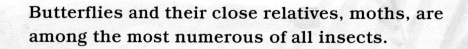

Butterflies and their close relatives, moths, are
among the most numerous of all insects.

Hmm. . . . Where could they be? This meadow is
usually all aflutter with butterflies.

While we're waiting for some butterflies to show up, why don't I tell you some things you should know about these critters.

BUTTERFLIES AND MOTHS BELONG TO THE ORDER OF INSECTS KNOWN AS LEPIDOPTERA.

LEPIDOPTERA MEANS "SCALED WINGS."

MICROSCOPIC SCALES GIVE BUTTERFLIES AND MOTHS THEIR BRILLIANT COLORS. WITHOUT SCALES, LEPIDOPTERA WOULD LOOK PALE AND GHOSTLY.

THE DELICATE SCALES RUB OFF LIKE POWDER.

BUTTERFLIES AND MOTHS HAVE THE SAME BASIC ANATOMY.

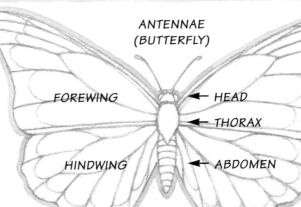

ANTENNAE (BUTTERFLY)

FOREWING

HEAD

THORAX

HINDWING

ABDOMEN

MOTH ANTENNAE ARE FEATHERY.

WHAT IS THE EASIEST WAY TO TELL A BUTTERFLY FROM A MOTH?

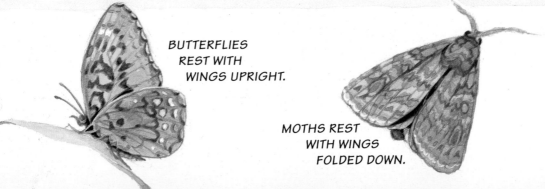

BUTTERFLIES REST WITH WINGS UPRIGHT.

MOTHS REST WITH WINGS FOLDED DOWN.

Hoo-hoo-hee! I was so busy talking, I didn't notice the monarch butterflies right here in my beard!

Monarchs are the best known of all butterflies. They are easily recognized by their bold pattern of orange and black.

*MONARCH BUTTERFLY*

The viceroy butterfly is the only other butterfly that resembles the monarch.

*VICEROY BUTTERFLY*

 *NOTE: THROUGHOUT THE BOOK, ALL BUTTERFLIES, MOTHS, AND CATERPILLARS ARE SHOWN ACTUAL SIZE.*

Monarchs and viceroys have bold yet simple
patterns that make them easy to recognize.
Here are more butterflies with simple
unmistakable patterns.

WHITE ADMIRAL →

RED ADMIRAL

ZEBRA LONGWING →

DIANA

MOURNING CLOAK

CALIFORNIA SISTER →

Follow me! I think I see a swallowtail butterfly
just over the knoll. Hurry!

ZEBRA
SWALLOWTAIL

It's fun to run after butterflies. But to get really
close, you have to approach slowly. Let's get a
good close-up look at these swallowtail
butterflies.

BLACK
SWALLOWTAIL

TIGER
SWALLOWTAIL

Swallowtails are my favorite butterflies. You can
recognize them by their long, swallowlike tails.

13

SWALLOWTAIL ON
QUEEN ANNE'S LACE

If you wait until a butterfly lands on a flower
and begins to feed, you can get quite close.
When a butterfly is sipping flower nectar, it pays
little attention to anything else. This
swallowtail is sipping from a wildflower called
Queen Anne's lace.

Butterflies and moths sip flower nectar and water through a long hollow tube called a proboscis.

Here are three other common wildflowers whose nectar butterflies seek out:

CLOVER

MILKWEED

PROBOSCIS

A PROBOSCIS CAN BE UNFURLED TO REACH NECTAR DEEP INSIDE ANY FLOWER.

THISTLE

NOTE: THISTLE PLANTS ARE PRICKLY ALL OVER. DO NOT TOUCH!

While you're looking for butterflies on a plant's flowers, look for butterfly caterpillars on the plant leaves. Every butterfly begins its life as a caterpillar.

The change from caterpillar to butterfly is called metamorphosis.

## THE LIFE CYCLE OF A BUTTERFLY

MONARCH EGG
(12X ITS ACTUAL SIZE)

A BUTTERFLY BEGINS LIFE IN THE EGG.

THE EGG HATCHES INTO A CATERPILLAR (LARVA). THE CATERPILLAR GROWS RAPIDLY FEEDING ON GREEN LEAVES.

MONARCH CATERPILLAR

AFTER IT HAS GROWN ALL IT CAN, THE CATERPILLAR CURLS UP AND FORMS A HARD-SHELLED CASE AROUND ITSELF CALLED A CHRYSALIS.

INSIDE THE CHRYSALIS, THE CATERPILLAR CHANGES INTO A BUTTERFLY. WHEN THE TIME IS RIGHT, THE BUTTERFLY BREAKS OUT, UNFURLS ITS WINGS, AND FLIES AWAY.

## HERE ARE THE CATERPILLARS OF THREE BUTTERFLIES YOU KNOW:

CALIFORNIA SISTER

BLACK SWALLOWTAIL

ZEBRA LONGWING

Not all butterflies are big and boldly patterned. Many butterflies are small and colored in soft pastel shades. Some are yellow or blue. Some are copper colored. And some butterflies are white.

ORANGE-BORDERED
BLUE

ACADIAN
HAIRSTREAK

CLOUDLESS SULPHUR

PURPLISH
COPPER

HERE ARE EIGHT LOVELY LITTLE
PASTEL-COLORED BUTTERFLIES
FOR YOU TO LOOK FOR:

CABBAGE WHITE

COMMON BLUE

ALFALFA BUTTERFLY

DOGFACE BUTTERFLY

19

Aha! Here are four butterflies we haven't seen yet. These have mottled or checkered color patterns.

Most butterflies can be found in sunny, open places, but a few species prefer the woods. Of the woodland butterflies, elfins and satyrs are my favorite.

PAINTED LADY

CHECKERED SKIPPER

CHECKERSPOT

CRESCENTSPOT

You have to look thoroughly to see woodland butterflies. Most are colored in browns and grays—just like the woods.

BROWN ELFIN

WOOD SATYR

NOTE HOW WOODLAND BUTTERFLIES BLEND INTO THEIR SURROUNDINGS.

21

Butterflies are daytime fliers. Moths fly mostly at night.

AT NIGHT, BUTTERFLIES SLEEP CLINGING
TO THE UNDERSIDE OF LEAVES.

Nobody knows exactly why night-flying moths are so strongly attracted to light, but because they are, moths are the easiest insects to locate.

MAPLE SPANWORM MOTH

DRIED LEAF MOTH

GYPSY MOTH

CUTWORM MOTH

DURING THE DAY, MOTHS SLEEP ON TREES OR BRUSH, CAMOUFLAGED AGAINST BARK.

Just turn on your porch light and dozens of moths will find you! You don't have to go any farther than your own doorstep.

GYPSY MOTH EGGS
IN SILKEN SAC

CATERPILLAR

PUPAL CASE (COCOON)
AND EMERGING WINGED
GYPSY MOTH

Like butterflies,
moths begin life in
the egg and hatch
as caterpillars.

ISABELLA MOTH AND
WOOLLY BEAR
CATERPILLAR

INCHWORM
AND GEOMETER MOTH

These two species of moths are better known
as caterpillars than as winged adults.

Depending on the species, moth caterpillars
eat plant leaves, stems, fruit, grain, flour, and
even clothing! As adults, moths feed mostly
on nectar, just as butterflies do.

Some moths are well known simply because of their large size. Here are five truly giant moths that may fly to your porch light:

POLYPHEMUS MOTH

BIG POPLAR SPHINX MOTH

These moths are so big that at first sight they might be a little scary. But don't be afraid—they're harmless.

REGAL MOTH

LUNA MOTH

CECROPIA MOTH

My favorite moths are called underwings. At rest, underwing moths are almost impossible to find. Their closed forewings blend perfectly with the bark of trees. But when they spread their wings, the brilliant colors of their underwings are revealed.

SWEETHEART UNDERWING

There are three underwing moths resting
on this tree's branches. See if you can
help Sassafrass find them.

Not all moths are night fliers. Three day-flying moths for you to keep an eye out for are the forester, ctenucha (pronounced *te-NOO-cha*), and hummingbird moth.

CTENUCHA (PRONOUNCED Te-NOO-cha) MOTH

FORESTER MOTH

HUMMINGBIRD MOTH

ACTUAL HUMMINGBIRD

It's morning, and the butterflies are awake. This has been a long walk. I should be tired, but I'm full of energy. I think I'll follow this old stone wall to see where it leads. Meanwhile, I hope you've enjoyed learning a little about the fascinating group of insects known as Lepidoptera. See you soon. Wave good-bye, Sassafrass. Bye!

HERE ARE MORE OF

## *Crinkleroot's*

NATURE GUIDES FOR YOU TO ENJOY:

Crinkleroot's Guide to Knowing the Birds
Crinkleroot's Guide to Knowing the Trees
Crinkleroot's Guide to Walking in Wild Places
Crinkleroot's 25 Mammals Every Child Should Know
Crinkleroot's 25 More Animals Every Child Should Know
Crinkleroot's 25 Birds Every Child Should Know
Crinkleroot's 25 Fish Every Child Should Know
I Was Born in a Tree and Raised by Bees
Crinkleroot's Book of Animal Tracking

32

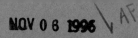